CONTENTS

Lizzie Brown

A Devonshire Pie Truck Mystery

Book One

A SLICE OF.... DEATH

Lizzie Brown

A Slice of Death

(C)2019 By Lizzie Brown

CHAPTER ONE

"**E**verything will be alright, sweetheart, I promise you that," Julia White said, stroking her daughter's long blonde hair as she sat beside her at the kitchen table.

It was the house Julia would never call home again, owing to the fact that she had recently gone through a hectic divorce and had decided she was long overdue a change. A change of scene, a change of hairstyle, even a change of job.

"But mum, are you sure you can pull off this pie truck business?" Kadi asked skeptically.

Julia looked at her eighteen year old daughter sideways. She couldn't pretend she wasn't a little bit offended by her remark. I mean, did she think she was a complete wreck? Although, having looked in the mirror that morning, she could well understand why she might be giving that impression. She looked like frump woman! "Hey, relax, will you? Of course I can pull it off. Besides, this is Devonshire we're talking about, not here in London. They're all for their pies there, you know?"

"I suppose," she replied, shrugging her shoulders.

"I know you'll miss me, but sweetheart, you have to stay here for your studies. You can come for a little holiday once I'm all settled in."

"I suppose." She sighed.

"So, now we've talked that one out, I'm off to get a hair cut and some new clothes. I'm going to be a whole new me, you'll see."

CHAPTER TWO

J ulia looked around the empty cottage. It was certainly quaint, but a quick glance out of the window revealed to her the tremendous views over the red sandstone cliffs the town of Budleigh Salterton was famed for.

She climbed the wooden staircase and stepped into the open plan bedroom, which was simple, but nice and airy and bright, owing to the skylight window in the ceiling. She checked the built in cupboards around the room, one of them proving to be a door leading into an ensuite washroom. "Very nice," she muttered. "Needs a lick of paint and a good dusting, but it will do nicely."

She was startled by a knock at the door and a voice calling to her from below. "Cooie! Anyone here?"

"Just a second!" She called, hurriedly checking her appearance in an old mirror left hanging on the wall by some previous owner. She smoothed down her new dark red, bob haircut that had got ruffled by the strong sea breeze outside and dashed down the stairs.

"Ah, you must be the new owner. I am your neighbour, Mrs Ivy Kinlaw," the old lady standing in her kitchen said. She had short, curly white hair, bushy eyebrows and a keen/sharp eye, grey in colour.

"Oh, is that so?" Julia asked, taken aback.

"I see you're from London."

"Ye-es, how did you know?"

"You're not used to being on intimate terms with your neighbours, plus the accent gives you away."

"That's right. I don't think any of the neighbours ever came to welcome us when we moved into the city."

There was a pause and Julia felt as though the older woman was waiting for her to speak.

"Oh, Julia White, by the way," she said, suddenly realising she had not yet introduced herself.

"Nice to met you. You'll have to get used to us here."

"I'm sure I'll love you all."

"Let us hope so. Is that your truck outside?" She asked, pointing outside to her red truck.

"Yes, I'm setting up a pie truck business."

"Ah, that puts us at odds to start with. I own the local cafe on the sea front. Make pies myself."

"Oh, I see."

Ivy narrowed her eyes at her. "Do you? I expect you'll be selling them at a competitive price?"

"Well, yes, but I only sell pies and you must sell much more at your cafe. It can't hurt to have a little competition, can it?"

Ivy was thoughtful and she seemed to be mulling this new idea over in her mind. "Good point." She shuffled on her feet. "Will you be at the local food fair next weekend?"

"Which food fair is that?"

"You don't know about it?"

"No, why don't you tell me about it over a nice cup of tea?"

"I'd better not, I've got to get on. You won't have the time to prepare pies for it, anyhow."

"Oh, I always have time to bake pies. I'm going to start work a.s.a.p. I have to. This place won't pay for itself."

"We know where we stand with each other, then. Let the battle commence."

"If that's what you want."

"May the best woman win."

CHAPTER THREE

J ulia parked her red truck in her allocated spot at the food fair. It was held in a spectacular spot, overlooking the bay. She got out the freshly baked pies and set them out, before opening the hatch.

"Let business and battle commence," she told herself, eyeing up Ivy Kinlaw's 'cafe creations' truck opposite.

Ivy waved to her from beneath the hatch and Julia waved back with a generous smile. She had to admit her food looked and smelled rather good. People were starting to come over already and they headed straight to Ivy, calling out a greeting to her. It seemed she had the advantage, being already established in the town.

She waited a long time before anyone came across. Her first customer proved to be a glamorous woman about ten years younger than herself, about thirty-five, wearing a bright pink jumper dress and purple leggings. Her face was heavily made up with both make-up and spray tan. "Hi, Ms Sapphire Stewart. You must be the Mrs White I've heard so much about," she said, tossing a few locks of shiny blonde hair over her shoulder as she extended her hand, revealing pointed pink nails.

Julia's chestnut coloured eyes widened in surprise. "You've heard of me?"

"Of course. There isn't much in this town that gets passed me, or any of us for that matter, but I forgot, you're from London, it's different there."

"I am and I prefer Ms too, if you don't mind? I reverted back to my maiden name after my divorce."

Sapphire placed a hand over her mouth. "Oh, I'm sorry. That must have sounded so insensitive."

"You weren't to know. Do you have anything to do with 'Sapphire Glam' in the high street?"

She giggled. "My boutique business, yes. You'll have to come by sometime, see what delights I can sell you."

"Well, what can I sell you, Ms Stewart?"

"You can call me Sapphire and I'll have whichever you recommend. They all look heavenly." She eyed them all closely as she was speaking.

"The cherry and almond is a new recipe and though I say so myself, it is rather good."

"Sounds perfect."

Julia cut a generous slice of the pie and placed it in front of Sapphire on a paper plate.

"It smells great. I think I'll try it right here, I'm enjoying our little chat," Sapphire said, sitting down on the high chair placed by the hatch.

"Me too. It's good to know I have a friend here."

"Mmmm, this is amazing pie!" Sapphire cried after swallowing a piece.

"You approve?"

"Oh, yes. I'll be buying pies from you more often."

"Don't tell Mrs Kinlaw, though," Julia whispered.

"Don't worry about her, she has a cafe to run."

"Hey, Sapphire! How's you?" A voice said from behind her.

Sapphire spun around on her chair, revealing the other woman to Julia's view. She was a smartly dressed professional looking woman, like a doctor or something. She was plain to look at with wiry brown hair in an nineteen eighties style and small, grey rimmed glasses. "Hey, Tegan! Long time no see!" Sapphire cried.

They embraced each other and then Sapphire introduced her to Julia. "This is my very good friend, Professor Tegan Smyth."

Julia looked at each woman in turn. Although

they were of a similar age, that is where their similarities ended and she couldn't quite believe they were friends. She looked at Sapphire for an explanation.

Sapphire giggled. "I see what you're thinking, but surprisingly enough, Tegan and I have got quite a lot in common."

Tegan smiled, revealing a row of perfect white teeth. "Though, obviously not science."

"We have been friends since high school. Tegan helped me with my science projects."

"That explains things. What field of science are you in?"

"Oh, Tegan works on medical formulas, she's working on something interesting at the moment."

"Hush, Sapphire, it's supposed to be top secret," Tegan gently scolded.

Sapphire placed a hand over her mouth. "Me and my big mouth. I'm sure Julia won't spread it about town."

Tegan looked at Julia for confirmation.

"I have no one to spread it too. I hardly know a soul."

"Of course. It's fine."

CHAPTER FOUR

It was a little later into the afternoon, when Julia was alone and awaiting more customers, when the fight broke out between Ivy Kinlaw and a bald man with a beer belly and a scowl on his face. He marched up to her truck and shouted out, "Ivy Kinlaw, you are a disgrace!" He pointed a finger at her all the while.

"You can say what you like. My pies are the best in all Budleigh Salterton."

A younger man came dashing over and stepped in, placing a hand on the fat man's shoulder and trying to drag him away. "Come away, uncle."

"I will not! It's outrageous! Charging such exorbitant prices for a pie that has gone off!"

"Might I remind you that you finished the whole pie, Mr Vallejo. You can't have a refund for that."

"Come away, uncle," his nephew repeated.

At last he yielded and moved away, fuming all the while. Julia picked out one of her best pies for him to try. "Try this, sir. It's on the house." She said, holding it up to him.

He wrinkled his nose and sniffed at the pie. Not a pretty sight. Then he waved it away. Connor took it out of Julia's hand and followed his uncle to try and persuade him to at least try it.

"I'll give it a try. Smells better than the last one." He took a huge bite and chewed on it thoughtfully. His face brightened and he finished it hungrily.

Julia looked across at Ivy triumphantly. Her gloating would be short lived, however, as Mr Vallejo pulled a face as he chewed on the last piece and muttered, "everything tastes foul today." He stormed away and Ivy gave Julia the thumbs up, followed by a huge grin.

"I'm so sorry about that, thanks for the thought," said his young nephew. "I'm Connor Clifton, by the way."

"Julia White. It seems I have some improving to do where your uncle is concerned." She watched the older man's retreating back with distaste.

"I'm sure they're delicious. My uncle is a tough nut to crack, I'm afraid." He ran a hand through his light brown hair, awkwardly.

"That's alright. I see he's not best pleased with Ivy Kinlaw, either." She laughed.

He turned to look at the old woman. "Good old Ivy. She's a tough nut too."

"Don't I know it. She's my biggest rival, as well as my neighbour."

He laughed. "You see, Julia, my uncle is a business man and he sees everything through the eyes of business. That is the only excuse I can offer for his behaviour."

"Well, then, that's settled, isn't it?"

"I'd better run," Connor said, watching his uncle's expectant face.

"Okay, but don't forget to call by my truck for lunch sometime!" She called after him.

"I won't!"

"Larry Vallejo? He's a businessman alright and a scoundrel," Sapphire Stuart said when Julia caught up with her again, during a short break from selling pies.

"You don't like him much, then?" Julia asked, nursing a mug of steaming hot chocolate between her hands to warm them.

"That's the biggest understatement of the year. Let's just say, he wouldn't be missed by many if he left town."

"Or died?" Julia suggested.

"Not even that."

"He didn't like my pies much, so I guess that makes him an enemy of mine too. His nephew seemed nice."

"Oh, so you've met the nephew?" Sapphire's eyes twinkled at the thought of him.

"I have. Are you sweet on him or something?"

"A little."

"He's a little too young for you and I, Sapphy. He would do for Kadi, however."

"Kadi?"

"My daughter, she's eighteen."

"Oh? Well, you'd better bring her here before someone snaps him up. Mind you, with an uncle like that..."

As if to add weight to her words a blood curdling scream reached them, coming from the direction of the beer tent, across from where they were standing. They both turned their heads in that direction.

CHAPTER FIVE

A s the two of them drew nearer to the beer tent, the cause of the commotion became apparent right away. Larry Vallejo's lifeless body was slumped over one of the tables and a young, geeky man was standing over him, apparently checking his pulse.

"Are you alright, Honey?" Sapphire called to the beer lady, Honey Dew, who was the dealer of the blood curdling scream they'd heard. She was too upset to speak and was crying on the shoulder of a male customer, her face smudged with make - up.

"Hey! Step back, would you, Ms Stuart?" The man checking the victim's pulse cried, sharply.

"Okay, calm down, Puck. We won't ruin your precious little crime scene."

"That's enough sarcasm from you, Ms Stuart and I'm back on duty, so it's P.C. Bird to you," the young man said.

Julia couldn't quite tell who he was speaking to as his eyes seemed to look right passed Sapphire.

"He's the law around here, is it any wonder people like Larry Vallejo can swan around the place causing havoc?" She whispered in Julia's ear.

"Hm, he seems like an interesting young man."

"Interesting, you call him? Weird, I say. He's always got his head in the clouds, a bit of a poet, I've been told."

"Is that right?"

"Is he dead, officer?" A voice behind them said.

Julia turned around to see Ivy Kinlaw hovering in the background.

P.C. Bird nodded. "I'm afraid so."

"What do you mean, you're afraid? No one liked him around here. You know that as well as any of us, Mr high and mighty," Ivy croaked.

Puck placed his hands upon his hips. "What has that to do with anything? He's still a dead body on our hands. By the way, did he eat anything from your truck, Ivy?"

"What are you suggesting? I poisoned him?"

"Who says he was poisoned?"

"Sounded like that was what you were implying."

Puck shrugged his shoulders. "It's possible,

though I didn't say it was deliberate."

Ivy puffed out her chest. "It wouldn't have been an accident if my food had anything to do with it," she said, looking at Julia.

Julia couldn't resist a dig back at her. "Oh, wouldn't it? Yet, I distinctly heard Mr Vallejo saying your pie tasted off."

"The man was crazy as well as crooked. I also heard him criticize your pie, Ms White and you offered it to him on the house."

Puck had been eyeing up Julia during this debate. "I haven't seen you before, are you new around these parts?"

"Julia White," she replied, holding out her hand to him. "I understand you're the law here?"

He waved away her hand and got out his notebook. "So, Ms White, you're saying Larry Vallejo didn't like the taste of Ivy's food?"

"I am."

"And you're not denying Ivy's claim that he also criticized the pie you offered him on the house?"

"And said it tasted foul," Ivy put in.

Julia shook her head, ignoring Ivy's comment. "Why should I deny it? I have nothing to hide. I didn't even know him," she answered.

He nodded. "That's if he was killed deliberately.

I'll get back to you on that one. I will have to check all the trucks before you clear them away." He warned. He got out his mobile and slowly walked away.

CHAPTER SIX

The next news that reached Julia was from the DCI himself, who called at her home a few days' later.

"Ms White?" Asked the tall, dark man with broad shoulders and a thinning hair line. He was a mature detective in his early fifties. He held up his police badge as he was speaking.

"That's me," Julia said, backing away from the door a little because of his brusque manner.

"Detective Chief Inspector Delbert Hewitt. I have come to take you to the local police station for questioning in regards to the murder of Mr Larry Vallejo. You don't have to say anything, but what you do say may harm your defense."

Julia gaped at him. "Excuse me. Am I being arrested?"

"Didn't you hear what I just said?"

"Oh, I heard you alright, Inspector. It is murder, then?"

"That's what I said."

"And you think I poisoned him with that slice of pie I gave him?"

"I know so. His nephew told us about your generosity in offering the pie on the house."

Julia folded her arms. "He also ate from Ivy Kinlaw's truck. What makes you suspect me, especially? What have you found?"

"We must carry on this discussion at the station. Only remember, I ask the questions."

"Yes, Inspector. I'll just get my coat."

"So, what do you have to say for yourself, Ms White?" Inspector Hewitt asked, his elbows resting on the table in an interview room, at the station.

Julia shivered and pulled her red mac coat tighter around her. This was serious. The findings at the lab proved that some pastry found left over in her fridge was laced with Arsenic. The same poison that was found in Larry Vallejo's blood stream. "I will only say one thing, I have no idea how Arsenic came to be in that pastry."

"None whatever?"

"None. Anyway, why would I poison a man I knew nothing about. I'd never even set eyes on him until the very same day he died."

He raised his eyebrows. "Sounds suspect to me."

"But what possible reason could I have?" She asked incredulously.

"That's what I have to find out. Men like Mr Vallejo get about a bit. You could have moved to town to get even with him about something in your past."

"What about Ivy Kinlaw? It's obvious she didn't like him very much."

"We have spoken to her and analysed the rubbish from her truck. There was no poison found anywhere near."

Julia sat back in her chair and mulled the events over in her mind. A sudden thought came to her. Something Larry Vallejo had said after he had eaten her pie. "Everything tastes foul today." She hadn't realized she'd said the words out loud, until the Inspector looked at her in surprise, expectantly waiting for an explanation.

"Oh, sorry, I was thinking aloud. That is what I heard Mr Vallejo say. Don't you think it's interesting?"

He shrugged. "I don't know."

"Well, in general terms it would imply that he had tasted something foul before he tasted my pie, wouldn't it? Something else must have tasted off before my pie," she explained.

The Inspector sighed. "This is pointless, Ms White. We have already found the source of the Arsenic and it was in your pastry."

"So? You have no proof it was me who put it there."

"Who else could have?"

"The real killer, of course."

"How would they do that?"

"They must have found a way. I did leave the truck unattended at times. Nobody thinks to lock up every time they take a break, not in a place like Budleigh Salterton."

"What are you saying?"

"You simply have no proof. I'm telling you it wasn't me, Inspector. I sample all my pies after they are baked and I'm still here to tell the tale. I think I've been framed and I don't have to look too far to know by whom."

He sighed and sat back in his chair. "It looks like you're right. We need more evidence." She could tell this was a hard pill for him to swallow.

"Thank you for being honest, anyway."

"You are free to go for now. Just don't leave town," he warned.

CHAPTER SEVEN

Aﬀter leaving the station, Julia marched along the high street and entered the 'Sapphire Glam' store, where Ms Stuart was serving a customer at the till. She smiled and waved as she placed an item of clothing into a carrier bag.

Julia browsed around the store at a few items while she waited for Sapphire to be free.

"That dress would suit you best, it's great with red hair," Sapphire said, once the customer had left. She waddled over to her and plucked the dress in question from its hanger. "Why not try it on?"

Julia took the garment from her hands and glanced at it more closely. It was a slimline dress in Black, with large, white polka dot patterns and a slim, red belt entwining the waist.

"Aren't I a bit old for this?" Julia asked.

"Of course not! My aunty bea bought one from me just last week and she's at least twenty years older than you are. Now go and try it on."

"Okay, I'll try it, but I'd love to see Kadi's face if she were here."

Sapphire laughed and Julia walked over to the changing room. She filled her friend in on the latest developments of Larry Vallejo's death through the curtain as she got changed.

After hearing Sapphire's exclamations of surprise and disgust in her many different forms, she said, "they really thinks it's you who poisoned him? You haven't lived here five minutes."

"That's what I tried to convince Hewitt of, but even though he let me off with a warning, somehow, I don't think it's over for me yet."

"What will you do?"

"There's only one thing I can do, I must find Larry Vallejo's killer myself." She threw aside the curtain after saying this and emerged looking like a whole new woman.

"Wow. Turn around," Sapphire said.

Julia turned in front of the free standing mirror and she had to admit, the dress was becoming, even for a forty-five year old.

Sapphire clapped her hands together in excitement. "It's simply stunning."

"I wouldn't go that far, but I do quite like it."

"Give me your phone." She held out her hand.

"Why?" Julia asked suspiciously.

"Nothing. I'm going to take a picture, that's all."

Julia sighed and reluctantly handed her mobile over. Sapphire took the picture with a giggle and started tapping away at the screen.

"What are you up to?"

"I've sent it to Kadi. I hope you don't mind?"

"Yes, I do mind, actually." She snatched her mobile back. "She'll have a good laugh at my expense."

"I'm sure she won't."

"We'll see. You don't know her like I do. She gets on with her father more than me. So you can guess whose side she was on after the divorce."

At that moment, her phone began to ring. It was Kadi. She signalled this to Sapphire who grinned and moved out of earshot, giving her some privacy.

"Hi, sweetheart," she said into the phone.

"Nice dress, mum. Where are you?"

"I'm still at the boutiques. Sapphire sent the pic."

"Sapphire?"

"Sapphire Stuart, she's the owner."

"Please tell me you're going to buy it."

Julia pulled a face, even though Kadi couldn't see her. "I thought you'd hate it."

"Why would I hate it, mum?"

"Anyway, something more serious has come up."

"What do you mean?" Her voice was wary.

"Don't worry, I haven't got a boyfriend or anything."

"That wouldn't bother me now."

"Wouldn't it? It's bad enough me dressing in young women's clothes."

"The dress looks great, mum."

"Thank you."

"What was the other business?"

Julia took a deep breath before plunging into an explanation of the events at the food fair and the police station.

"Cool." Was all Kadi could say.

Julia pulled the phone away from her ear for a moment and looked at it in disbelief because of what she was hearing down the other end. "It's not cool from where I'm looking. I could go to prison if I don't find out who killed the guy."

"Really? You're not a killer," she scoffed.

"Just this once I'm glad of your negative appraisal of my character. Try telling that to the police."

"I'm coming over," Kadi said with determination.

"No! What about your studies?"

"Oh, I can catch up with them."

"It's not necessary, I can handle this."

"Mum, you need me more than my studies do. You're not going to make me change my mind."

CHAPTER EIGHT

K adi arrived at Julia's cottage the very next morning and straight away she expressed her disapproval of the arrangements.

"Couldn't you modernize it?" She asked, her wide blue eyes darting around the living room.

Julia pursed her lips. "Hardly. It's an old cottage, modern just wouldn't look right."

"Well, it sure needs something," Kadi replied, shaking her head.

"That's enough cheek from you, young lady. Go and get washed and changed and we can dine out tonight."

"Like where? I've just come through the town and there ain't much to see."

"I know just the place. Ivy Kinlaw's cafe."

"That's the neighbour you were telling me about?"

"That's the one."

"Why would you want to go there?"

"Because, I suspect she is hiding something about Larry Vallejo. I'm not convinced the bad tasting pie was the only quibble she'd had with him."

"Oh, I see. That'll be fun."

The cafe was deserted as it was a little too early in the evening for most people, but that better suited Julia's purpose as she was more likely to get Ivy to talk about the fair.

Ivy, who was seated at one of the nearby tables, looked up from the magazine she was reading as they entered. She seemed surprised to see Julia. "Ah, Ms White. Come to set the record straight, have you?" She mocked.

"No, my mum has done nothing wrong!" Kadi said.

Julia smiled at Kadi's defense of her when she knew the next minute she would be at her throat again. "This is my daughter, Kadi. She has come to stay with me until I can get back on my feet again. We would like to see the menu, please."

Ivy got to her feet and shuffled towards the pile of menus on the counter, by the till. She selected two and handed one to each of them. "Take a seat. I'll be right over to take your orders." She said mechanically and then disappeared into the kitchen.

Kadi looked worriedly towards the door. "Are you sure you want to eat here, mum? As you suspect her of a poisoning?"

"Don't be silly. She isn't going to poison us. She would have had a very good motive for poisoning Mr Vallejo and she's too smart to try it again. That would give the game away too easily."

Kadi shrugged her shoulders. "I suppose you're right."

They found a seat in a booth by the window and Ivy came to take their orders.

"Now, what can I get you?" She asked, pen poised to pad.

"I'll have the vegan burger and sweet potato fries, please and also a chocolate milkshake," Kadi said, reading from the menu.

Ivy noted this down and turned to Julia.

"I'll just have the Caesar salad and a lemonade."

"Coming right up," she chuntered, shuffling back into the kitchen.

Kadi leaned forward and whispered, "I think she's strange. It's freaking me out." She shivered.

"Strange enough to be our killer?" Julia whispered back.

Kadi nodded. "Hey! Why don't I put her profile

up." She took her mobile out of her coat pocket.

Julia gave her a look of skepticism. "I doubt she knows what a profile is, never mind has one."

"Oh, I suppose not. Well, what about the Vallejo guy?"

"Mm, he was a businessman."

"Yeah, there's bound to be something on him." She began punching letters on the screen.

"It seems nobody here liked him, that could be the simple motive."

"You think it's more, though, with Ivy, right?"

Julia nodded.

"Hey! Here we are." Kadi turned the mobile screen to face her mum. "This is his business website."

Julia took the phone from her and read the screen. 'Vallejo's Land Agency' was the business name. "Hm. Seems like he owned a lot of the business properties around here, or at least the land."

Kadi looked around the cafe. "Do you think he owned this place?"

"It's possible. I could ask Ivy."

Right on cue, the kitchen door flew open and Ivy came out with their food.

"You know, a little bird told me that Larry Vallejo owned this cafe, is that true?" Julia asked casually, as Ivy placed the bowl of salad in front of her.

Ivy gave her a somewhat sour look. "He owned the land, that's all. I built this business myself. He isn't going to take credit for that." She said, putting a huge plate of burger and fries in front of Kadi.

"I'm sure, but how were things with the land?"

"What are you suggesting? That I poisoned Larry because business wasn't going so well?" Her hands flew to her hips, indignantly.

"Not especially. I'm just curious about the man I've been accused of murdering. Was he good to do business with?"

She threw her head back. "Ha! He was a scoundrel."

"Oh, really. Why do you say that?"

"He just was."

"How about his nephew, Connor? I was speaking to him at the fair. He seems nice."

"Yes, a nice enough lad. I expect he'll take over the business now."

"Was Mr Vallejo a regular customer, Mrs Kinlaw?" Kadi asked.

"Yes, he was. I saw him in here on a number of occasions," another voice said from the direction of the door. It was P.C. Bird, still in uniform.

Ivy turned around to face him. "Evening, officer.

The usual, is it?"

"Yes, thanks, Ivy."

Ivy went back into the kitchen and Puck strolled over to their table. "So, you think of yourself as quite the detective, do you?" He asked, propping up the table next to theirs.

"Not really. I would like to clear my name, though."

He folded his arms. "That's if you're innocent."

"Of course she is!" Kadi exclaimed.

"My daughter, Kadi."

"Ah, she's living with you now?"

"On a temporary basis."

"Well, a word of advice, Ms White. Leave the detective work to the professionals. My boss doesn't have to know about this if you desist now." He walked away before she could reply to this and found a table as far away from theirs as possible.

CHAPTER NINE

The next morning, Julia set up her truck, even though she didn't expect to get many customers. The exceptions were, of course, Sapphire Stuart and her friend Professor Smyth, who both ate their lunch there.

"I didn't know Larry owned most of the land around here," Julia said, as Sapphire and Tegan tucked into a meat and potato pie each.

"Didn't I say?" Sapphire asked.

"You said he was a businessman."

"Oh, that's right, I was about to tell you when Honey Dew screamed and interrupted us."

"He owned my lab. The business and the land, so I had to see more of him than I'd have liked," Tegan said, rolling her eyes.

"So, Connor would own your business now?"

"That's correct, though I haven't seen him since

his uncle's death."

Julia became thoughtful.

"What are you thinking? That Connor killed his uncle to get his hands on the land?" Sapphire asked.

"I don't like to accuse him, yet, you have to admit it is plausable."

Sapphire pursed her lips. "It would be if he was not such a charming, handsome young man and a possible to marry your daughter off to."

"Don't tease, I don't think Kadi would like to hear you say so. He does seem too charming to be a killer, though, you're right there."

"He's rich too," Sapphire said.

"His list of good qualities are growing by the minute," Tegan said.

"What's puzzling me, is how he could have administered the poison," Julia said.

"That's the tricky bit," Sapphire said slowly.

"I suppose he could have put the poison in the pie when he handed it to his uncle," Julia said.

"And then came back and poisoned the pastry during all the commotion," Tegan said.

"That could have been how it happened," Julia said.

"That scream from Honey would have given anyone a good cover. Hey, wait, did you notice how

Ivy came along later?" Sapphire asked, suddenly.

"True." Julia was thoughtful for a moment. "I still can't help but think that the key to all this is Larry's own statement, that 'everything tastes foul today.' I wonder if he ate something before Ivy's pie."

"So it was someone else who poisoned him?" Sapphire asked. "But who?"

"I'll have to get back to you on that one."

Julia was surprised, when a little later in the day, she had a visit to her truck by the DCI himself. He leaned on the truck and fixed her with a stony stare.

"Afternoon, Inspector, what can I get you?" Julia asked with a friendly smile.

"Nothing from this truck. I just stopped by to inform you that you cannot be selling pies while you are under investigation for poisoning Mr Vallejo. You must close up until this case is under wraps."

Julia folded her arms. "Just what am I supposed to do in the meantime?"

He waved a disinterested hand in her direction. "That's your affair. Just close this truck down, Ms White. It's for your own good."

Fuming to the DCI's retreating back, Julia began to pack things away with a little more force than was necessary. "Well, officer, I am going to wrap this case up myself and sooner than you think."

CHAPTER TEN

With plenty of time on her hands now the truck business was temporarily at an end, Julia called in at Larry Vallejo's mansion on the outskirts of the town, where his office had been located and where she hoped to find Connor.

The cleaning lady answered the door and she escorted Julia to the office, where she told her Conner was, at that moment, organising the paperwork.

"Hello, Julia!" Connor said cheerily when he saw her. "As you can see, my uncle didn't leave things in a very organised state."

Julia looked around at the disarray in the room. "I can see that. I didn't think you'd want to speak to me."

"Because I think you killed him?" Conner asked, standing up from the chair, behind the desk.

"Well...yes, actually."

"Why would that bother me? Whoever killed him did me a favour."

"Oh." Julia was a little stunned by this confession.

He held up his hands. "I didn't kill him, though and I don't think you did, either."

"That's good to know."

"I expect you want to find out who did?"

"Yes, that's why I'm here." To gain his trust, she felt she needed to put on a show of being open with him about her investigation.

"Well, if it wasn't you or me, then who was it?"

"That's the big question. I was hoping you could give me some idea."

"Right, let me think. Ivy Kinlaw?"

Julia looked surprised. "What makes you say that?"

"You do suspect her, though, don't you?"

"I did. However, I think your uncle ate somewhere else before Ivy's truck."

He ran a hand through his hair as she'd seen him doing at the fair. She decided this was his awkward pose.

"I don't know about that. However, I did find these." He waved a wad of papers in front of her face. "Which, I think you might be interested to see."

He handed the papers over and Julia perused them, thoughtfully.

"He was going to sell her cafe?" She asked when she had read them.

"That's about the sum of it, yes. He wanted to sell the land, because, as you can see from those papers, business was struggling. It still is, as-a-matter-of-fact. I'm muddling my way through the best I can, that's why I'm here."

"It gives her a stronger motive than I'd at first thought." Julia chewed over this new information for a moment. "Are you certain your uncle didn't have anything else to eat at the fair?"

"No, I'm not. I..err...let me think..." He broke off.

"Did he comment about anything else tasting foul?"

"Ye-es, there was something..." He broke off again. "That's it!"

Julia almost jumped out of her skin at this sudden outburst.

"The beer tent! He had a pork pie there, or at least he tasted it and then struck up an argument with Honey Dew about it's tasting funny. Then he threw the rest in the bin. He liked his pastry, my uncle, hence his size."

"Ah, I see, and then paranoia struck in and he thought everything tasted horrible thereafter. It was Honey who found the body and it is usually the one who finds the body who committed the crime. It's a shame the rubbish from the fair would have gone to the incinerator by now."

"You sound like you know your stuff," he said with a grin.

"Not really. I'm just desperate to clear my name, is all. What do you know about Honey Dew?"

He shrugged. "She worked at the local pub."

"Was your uncle a regular?"

"Oh, yes. He liked a pint."

"It makes you wonder why he went back to the beer tent later."

"It doesn't surprise me. He couldn't resist."

Julia glanced up at a picture of Larry on the wall, with two heavily made up women at either side of him. "It seems to me that your uncle was a typical businessman and I wonder...Honey beeing, you know, that type, whether they were involved."

Connor followed her glance and grinned. "You could say that, but I can't speak for Honey."

CHAPTER ELEVEN

Honey was pulling a pint when Julia entered the pub that evening, along with Kadi and she requested a word with her during her break, as she ordered a soda water for herself and a shandy for Kadi.

Julia observed the bar maid from their table and it was safe to say she was a persistent flirt. That would have caught Larry's eye for sure.

"Mum, there's something I wanted to talk to you about," Kadi said, drawing her attention away from Honey.

"This sounds serious," Julia answered, warily.

"It is serious, for you and for me."

"Oh, yeah. Tell me, then?"

"Well, you see, I've met someone." She lowered her eyes.

"Someone?" Julia raised her eyebrows.

"He's called Elliot Chance and his dad is about your age, who's single. He's called Clyde."

"I see where this is heading. You're trying to set me up."

"He's awfully nice and good looking for a man of that age."

"That age?" Julia rolled her eyes.

"Well, you know." She raised her shoulders.

"Where did you meet this Elliot?"

"At the beach. He asked me to lunch at his house and that's where I met Clyde. I was telling him about you and how you needed a man about the house."

Julia giggled. "That was forward of you. You really think I need a man?"

She nodded. "I think you do, yes. It'll do you good to go out for a change. You can wear that new dress you bought from Sapphire's boutique."

"Hang on. You haven't arranged anything?"

Kadi looked sheepish.

"Oh, Kadi, you didn't? I can't go."

"Why not?"

"I'm in the middle of trying to prove my innocence in a murder investigation. One thing at a time, please."

"It will take your mind off it for a while. It's

already arranged now, there's no going back, he's booked a table for you."

"Oh, please. You could have asked me first."

"Will you go?" Kadi asked, wrapping her hair around her little finger.

"I'll have to think about it. Here comes Honey."

Honey sat beside Julia at her invitation and chewed gum while they talked.

"Yeah, he was a sleazebag, was Larry. We went out a couple of times. He was very rich, that's what attracted me, I think." She pulled down her leopard print top as she was speaking.

"Then you fell out?"

"I'd had enough. I get bored easy and he wasn't a nice man to be around. He bought me some nice jewellery, though." She fiddled with an expensive looking necklace she was wearing. "He let me keep some of it."

"He ate a pork pie from your tent, so Connor said?'

"He ate a little and then he kicked off about how it tasted funny. It was a hot day, so I guess it could have been off, though I think he was just trying to make trouble for me and scare some of the customers away. There was no poison in them."

"Did he say anything when he came back for a pint?"

"No, but he looked ill. He was rather pale and he was slouching at the table. Then, he just flopped on his face all of a sudden. I went over to see if he was okay and he was...." She broke off and shuddered.

"Did Ivy Kinlaw visit your tent?"

"That old crow? Yes, I remember her and Larry seemed to be having a heated discussion at the table at some point during the day."

"When was this?"

She looked up at the ceiling while she thought about the question for a moment. "I don't remember exactly, it was very busy. I think it was after Larry came into the tent the first time."

"That's interesting."

Honey went back to the bar and Julia turned back to Kadi. "Well, I've learnt that it could have been Honey who poisoned Larry, but that Ivy Kinlaw is still in the running. She could have slipped in and poisoned the pork pie while she was arguing with Larry."

"You think the poison took all that time to take effect?"

"Yes, it could have. It wasn't a very long time."

"Then Ivy poisoned your pastry to frame you?"

"Yes, and to close down my truck business. So far it's worked, too."

"That was her secondary motive, then."

Julia nodded. "No doubt she had been planning this poisoning for a long time before the fair and, at the very moment we became rivals, it must have entered her head to use me as scapegoat."

"How dare she!"

"I'm going to have it out with her." And so saying, she called round at Ivy's cottage after they got home from the pub.

The old woman was busy baking cakes for her cafe and she had her back to Julia, bending over the oven as she placed a couple of cake tins inside.

The kitchen door stood open ajar and Julia popped her head through and called, "cooie!" Just as Ivy had done to her on her first day at the cottage. Ivy nearly jumped out of her skin and she spun around. "You frightened me half to death." She said under her breath.

"Well, we're not in London now, as you so kindly informed me earlier."

"No, we're not," she replied with distaste. She slammed the oven door shut to show her annoyance at this unwelcome interruption. "Why are you here?" She asked unkindly.

"To talk about the quarrel between you and Larry at the beer tent."

"Who says I was there?"

"Honey does."

"Well, she's a liar, trying to pass the book."

"What do you mean? You think Honey did it?"

"She had a quarrel with him herself, putting it mildly. It was more like a blazing row."

"Where?"

"Outside the tent. I was milling around and Honey scowled at me when I asked her if everything was alright."

"That would explain why she sounded so annoyed about you being around."

She let out a cackling laugh. "Annoyed, was she? I'd say so."

"Can you remember what the quarrel was about?"

She nodded. "I presume you know they were involved?"

"Yes, she told me that much."

"Well, it sounded like he was throwing her over. He said he could no longer afford to keep her."

"But she wanted him to stay?"

"For the jewellery, no doubt. She has an expensive taste, that girl."

"It's funny, she said it was the other way around and she was the one who got bored. I suppose it was because Larry's business was struggling."

CHAPTER TWELVE

I t was the evening when she was supposed to join Clyde Chance for dinner and Julia was still in two minds as to whether she should go or not. She kept on trying to find excuses, to which, Kadi kept coming up with smart answers why she should go.

"You do realise that if it comes to anything with me and Mr Chance, then Elliot will be your step brother?" She asked, sitting on the sofa in her dressing gown and with her hair all wet.

Kadi rolled her eyes. "I keep telling you, Elliot and I are just friends."

"So that wouldn't bother you?"

"No. You have to go, anyway. It's only half an hour before you have to meet him at the restaurant." Kadi looked at her watch.

"Alright, you win," she replied, standing up and moving towards the stairs. She paused with her foot on the first step and turned around. "You don't think he'll be annoyed that I chose to meet him there, do you? Some men don't like their women too independent."

Kadi threw a cushion at her. "Just go!"

Julia milled her way through the busy, seafood restaurant, located just outside town. She stopped at the bar to get a distant look at the man she was about to meet for the first time. The waitress had pointed him out to her.

It was true he was good-looking, with his shiny locks of golden brown hair and a neatly trimmed beard, and there seemed to be a particular charm about him, even from this distance. He had dressed carefully in a crisp, grey suit and white shirt and he even sported a red bow tie, which you didn't see too often these days'. He seemed so cool and collected sitting there, that he could almost have been a spy. She hoped not!

When she got to the table, he looked up at her with the brown sugar eyes he had and a smile broke out on his lips, revealing perfect white teeth. She had already convinced herself that they had very little in common at this moment, but she was here now and he'd seen her, so she had to go ahead with it.

"You must be Julia. I've heard so much about you from Kadi, that I would have recognised you without arranging a meeting." His voice was soft and friendly, not what she was expecting at all. Perhaps appearances were deceptive.

She sat down opposite him. "Oh, dear. I hope she hasn't told you too much." She said.

"I'm sure there's nothing too terrible to tell." He handed her a menu.

"She hasn't told you, then?" She opened the menu and peered at him from over the top.

"If you mean about the murder, I know everything. I used to work with Larry. I dabble in land agency, you see?"

"Eek," Julia said, swallowing hard.

"I didn't like him, though. I'm not of his sort, I hope you understand?"

"If you mean a womaniser, I'm glad to hear it because you'd be wasting your time with me if you were."

"My one and only wife died five years ago."

"Oh, I'm sorry to hear that."

"It's alright. I've come to terms with it now. How about you?"

"You mean the divorce?"

He nodded, looking his sympathy.

She waved an unconcerned hand. "I'd better not attempt that subject right now, though, I am well over him and it was his fault, whatever Kadi thinks.

It's just so messy and compromised."

"I'm sure Kadi doesn't blame you."

"No, she knows her dad was at fault. He is the one living with another woman, after all. She just dotes on her dad and we have never really seen eye to eye."

"It can be like that with mother and daughter relationships."

"Swiftly moving on, what can you tell me about Larry Vallejo?"

"What would you like to know?"

"What was he like to work with?"

"Oh, Larry was as corrupt as they come and he upset a lot of people, including myself."

The waitress came back to their table and they placed their orders. She poured champagne into their glasses and left them in peace.

"Is there anything you can tell me about any particular business interests of Larry's?" Julia asked.

Clyde thought for a moment. "I believe his latest thing was a sudden turn for science."

Julia's eyes widened. "That's right. He owned Tegan Smyth's lab."

"Yes, apparently Tegan was working on something that captured his interest."

"Yes, I remember Tegan saying something about

that, but she said it was top secret."

"It would have been a secret to most people, but somehow Larry had got wind of it. It was his business."

"And he spoke to you about it?"

"Yes, Tegan wasn't too happy about her work being spoken about."

"Could that have been a big enough motive to murder him? She is a scientist who would probably be able to get hold of Arsenic."

"How would she have administered it? It must have been given him at the fair."

"Oh, yes. It was definitely given to him at the fair."

"Yet, then again, there could be more to this case than meets the eye."

Julia looked surprised.

"Things are not always as they appear," he explained.

"You're getting complicated."

"Could it be that there is a simpler explanation out there than you think?"

Julia frowned, puzzled. "How can there be?"

"As we are on the subject of science, you need to find the winning formula," he replied, tapping the side of his nose.

CHAPTER THIRTEEN

If only she could 'find the winning formula,' as Clyde had said. There was only one thing for it. She needed to look for clues. The police didn't seem to be making too much headway there, although they wouldn't have informed her of their findings if they had.

She reached over her bed, where she had been sitting thinking things over and found a notepad in the drawer of her bedroom cabinet and began jotting down the story so far.

She now had four suspects, thanks to Clyde. Kadi had told her it was worth dating him for that.

Ivy Kinlaw had the most motive and opportunity to poison Larry and she did seem to be omitting something from her story. Had she been lying that she didn't quarrel with Larry in the beer tent?

Then there was his nephew Connor Clifton, who made it no secret that he wasn't sorry his uncle was dead and would take over the business. He also had opportunity to slip the poison into the pie his uncle ate from her truck. Yet, would he really want to take over the business while it was in such disarray? Was he really too charming to do the deed? Or was his charm a good cover for it?

Honey could have had a blazing row with Larry as Ivy had said and killed him on the spur of the moment, out of anger. Or was her motive for the crime because Larry had threatened to take back the jewellery? Business was struggling and he would need all the financial help he could get.

And now there was Tegan. She hated to say it, as she was Sapphire's friend, though she didn't have an opportunity to administer the poison, even though she would have the means to obtain it. Was his interfering with her business and speaking about it a good motive for murder? Would she have risked it all for that?

Julia frowned and shook her head while writing this last question. She didn't think so, but she could ask Tegan about winning formulas.

She put away the notepad and after switching off the bedside lamp, settled down to sleep.

She pulled up outside Tegan's lab the next morning and sauntered threw the sliding doors into a white and cleanly foyer area, with a shiny, white marble floor you could almost see your reflection in.

She walked up to the reception area, where a curly haired man, wearing glasses and dressed in a long, white coat was busy typing away on his computer. The badge on his coat bore his name: Professor Tim Wilby.

She waited for him to look up and then said, "good morning. Is it possible to speak to Professor Tegan Smyth?"

He had a serious face and he didn't crack a smile as he silently observed her. "Professor Smyth is very busy. I can't let you through to the lab unless you have an appointment." His voice sounded mechanical.

"I don't have an appointment, but I know Tegan and she will see me. Tell her it's Ms White and I want to talk more about Larry Vallejo."

Tim raised an eyebrow at the mention of Larry. "I'll tell her you're here." He said, standing from behind the desk.

A little later Tegan came out to her wearing a white coat and a pair of goggles on top of her head. "Julia! I am surprised to see you." She said, embracing her with an air kiss.

"This isn't a social call, I'm afraid," Julia said, biting her lip. "I need to talk to you about..."

"Larry, I know," Tegan interrupted. "Come into my office."

She followed her down the corridor and into her office, which was as neat and tidy as she expected.

"I told you Larry owned the business," Tegan began, motioning for her to have a seat. Julia complied and sat down on the nearest chair, while Tegan perched on the edge of the desk.

"That's right, only I've found out recently that his business was struggling, somewhat. How did that affect you at the lab?"

Tegan folded her arms and nodded slowly. "We're doing okay. I've invested my own money into this place, as has Tim."

"I see. You mentioned you were working on something at the moment, are you at liberty to tell me a little about it."

"Oh, that. It's nothing really. Sapphire exaggerates, as you've probably already found out."

Julia laughed, though the hesitation in Tegan's voice hadn't gone unnoticed by her.

"The work we do here is very beneficial to the medical field, however," she added quickly.

"Very," Julia said with conviction. She then switched to a more casual approach as she asked, "I hear Larry had taken a sudden turn for science, himself."

"Where did you hear that?" She asked sharply.

"Oh, don't worry. I know everything has to be top secret, it's just a friend who worked with him sometimes said he seemed enthusiastic all of a sudden and it was unlike him."

Tegan sighed and rubbed her ankle. "It was unlike him. He only cared about money." She walked to the door and opened it, leaving her hand resting on the side.

"Well, I'll leave you to it."

"Would you like a tour before you leave?"

"No, I'd better be off. I don't want to interrupt your work any longer."

CHAPTER FOURTEEN

As Julia walked to her car from the lab, it was the phrase, 'he only cared about money,' that stuck in her mind. Had he demanded more money for the land and from the business? She had sounded angry about it. Why his sudden turn for science? Tegan had seemed to evade this question.

"It couldn't have been her," Julia muttered over and over as she drove home. "There was no way she could have poisoned him without injecting him, and the post mortem would have shown that up." She exhaled with relief. "Thank goodness I don't have to tell Sapphire I suspect her friend. She would never forgive me."

She was nearly home when she saw Connor Clifton's car coming towards her on the opposite side and she was amazed when she saw who he had as passenger.

It was Honey Dew!

She quickly turned the car around and followed at a safe distance. To her surprise, they drove past Larry's mansion and continued on the main road out of Budliegh Salterton. She continued following them until they arrived in the next village, where he turned off into a side street and parked up. Julia sailed on by and pulled into the next turning, leaving the car parked behind a bush and peeped out from behind the shop she had parked next to.

Connor and Honey emerged from behind the office they had parked by and went inside. Julia was still reeling from the shock of seeing Honey dressed smartly, in a blue business suit and a silky cream blouse. Something wasn't right here!

Going round the back way, instead of by the road, she discreetly managed to peer through the window and into the office of the man Connor was about to do business with. The window was slightly ajar so she could here everything being said, as well as observe.

It was quite extraordinary to Julia how Honey had a sudden turn for business, a bit like Larry with his science. Just what was going on here? Could this have been 'the winning formula,' so to speak? The way of looking at this mystery through the eyes of Clyde Chance?

It was clear to her that both Connor and Honey were not as they had seemed. Certainly not the way they had presented themselves. From the conversation that ensued, she gathered they were hustlers of unsuspecting business men.

"Yes, I am his nephew. The business he left me upon his sad and untimely demise, is going swimmingly, which means I am in a position to invest in your business."

"I heard he was murdered," the business man said.

"That's right, they found his killer. Some mad woman poisoned him with one of her pies at the food fair we attended."

Julia huffed. "Mad woman, indeed! So, that's what you think of me, is it?"

"How tragic."

She had seen enough. There was just one other thing to do and then she was off. She took out her mobile and discreetly snapped a picture of the three of them.

Julia ran back to her car and made straight for Larry's mansion, while Connor was otherwise engaged. She knew the cleaning lady wouldn't be there at that time of day, she just needed to find a way of breaking into the office, unobserved.

She left her car down the country lane that ran along side the house and walked to it, looking over her shoulder to check nobody was about, before she stepped onto the gravel drive. She was then out of sight and could be free to do some snooping around for a possible break-in opportunity.

As she went around the back, she noticed there was a flat roof, underneath the window to the office. If she could get passed the drain pipe hurdle, she might just be able to climb up and find a way of opening the window. She reached out and checked how sturdy it was. It seemed stable enough, so holding her breath, she attempted the climb.

Once she got level with the roof, she just about managed to scramble up. She rubbed her sore hands and examined the window. It was open ajar, but as she pushed on it, found it was locked. She pushed harder, breaking the lock. "Sorry for breaking your window, Connor. I will pay for the damage later. It's all in a good cause." She muttered as she climbed inside the office.

She rushed over to the desk and examined all the drawers one by one. Eventually, she found the proof she was looking for. There was a wad of files, all filled with forged documents belonging to different business' in the area. The business' had invested lots of money into Larry's land agency, much to their great loss, as the business was clearly in jeopardy.

"This must have been Connor and Honey's plan, to kill Larry and then take over the business and then get other business' to invest money, before they knew it was in trouble. Then escape with the dosh."

She heard the front door close downstairs and with her heart pounding, she tucked a few of the more important documents inside her coat pocket and flew to the window. Hearing footsteps getting closer to the office, however, she found there was no time to get back out of the window. She closed it, to hide the broken lock and clambered under the desk, just as the office door opened and Connor and Honey appeared in the doorway.

CHAPTER FIFTEEN

T hey were both laughing as they entered the room and then Connor grabbed Honey by the waist and pulled her into his arms. "You were brilliant, Hon. Just as you were with uncle. I knew your charm and good looks would be worth investing in." He said.

She threw her head back and laughed. "Yes, I do play the role of a brain dead bimbo, quite well, don't I?"

"And you're having dinner with him tonight?"

"Yes, the poor fool." She leaned towards him and he kissed her.

Julia was suddenly distracted by something blue in her peripheral vision. She looked down at the cream carpet. There was definitely something blue underneath one of the desks legs. It looked like a spilled liquid of some sort. Something scientific, perhaps?

She tugged at a few pieces of stained carpet, sticking out from under the leg and a few strands came away. She tucked them into her pocket, along with the documents and carried on watching the scene unfolding in front of her.

Connor had moved closer to the desk. She could see his shining black shoes. Her breath caught as she knew the game was up if he pulled out the desk chair. To her relief, though, he stayed standing up as he opened the drawer on the left and began to root around.

"Is everything ready?" Honey asked.

"Yes, everything's here, along with the passports. After your little dinner tonight, we'll be ready to go."

"I'd best go and find something to wear."

"You'll look wonderful in whatever you wear."

Julia felt she could breath again as they made for the door, when the unthinkable happened. She let out a big sneeze! It must have been the carpet fibers!

Connor and Honey stopped dead and looked at each other.

"Did you hear that?" Connor asked.

"Yes, it sounded like a sneeze."

Connor ran to the desk and peered underneath. A big grin overspread his face as he recognised her.

"Well, if it isn't Julia? Come on out." He said.

"You?" Honey cried as she appeared from under the desk.

Julia looked sheepish. "Sorry, I had to break-in. I know everything. I followed you to the office today." She explained.

"Well, you might as well hear the rest," Connor said, still in his charming tone.

Honey shot him a warning look.

"It's alright, Hon. We'll be long gone before the police hear about it. You might as well forget the dinner tonight. Get our passports ready."

"The police?" Julia asked warily.

Connor ran a hand through his hair and with his mobile at the ready, blocked the door. "That's right. I'm calling the police to report the break-in. They'll find you here and we'll go on a little journey. They will assume you broke in to destroy some evidence of your involvement in Larry's death."

"I have these!" Julia cried, panic in her voice, as she held up the documents she'd taken from the desk.

Connor laughed. "I assume they are proof we tried to con my uncle. Well, it turns out we didn't have to, he left me the business by conveniently dying."

"Very conveniently. You poisoned him to get

your hands on the business. That's why you told me that whoever killed him did you a favour."

"Exactly, that's why I didn't have to. Think about this for a moment, Julia. If you were any kind of detective you would have worked out that we were going to get the business anyway, without poisoning him," he scoffed.

"Too right. We do this kind of thing all the time. We never kill anyone," Honey said with a laugh.

Julia had to admit they were right and the documents didn't prove anything, apart from the fact that they were con artists. The police would never buy it. "I am going to tell the police about the hustling, so if they arrest me, I'm taking you down with me." She threatened.

"Oh, we can just slip away before the police arrive," Honey said.

"It looks like the game is up. You're going to go to prison for my uncle's death and there's nothing you can do about it."

CHAPTER SIXTEEN

J ulia looked around the cold cell she was being
kept in until her interview, and shivered. She
had really messed up. Why had she been so convinced the hustling was proof that Connor killed
Larry? She had hit a brick wall and couldn't see a
way out.

The police had found her alone at the house
after Connor and Honey escaped out of the window
she had broken, just as the sirens sounded. They got
away out of the back gate and Julia had no time to
escape and even if she had, running was only going
to make her look even more guilty.

Her only hope now, it seemed, was Clyde
Chance. She had phoned Kadi to let her know what
had happened and she promised to call Clyde. She
hadn't the foggiest what he would do. No doubt he'd
want to be her knight in shining armour.

The cell door opened with a clang and P.C. Puck Bird came in, jangling the keys in his hand. "This way, Ms White." He said with a triumphant grin.

"It's alright, you grinning. You didn't come up with much more yourself," Julia said with sarcasm in her tone. "You'd do better if you came down from cloud nine, once in a while." She continued as he walked her to the interview room.

"Save it for the DCI, Julia," Puck said, swinging open the door.

He followed her in and ushered her over to the waiting detective who pulled out a chair for her at the other end of the table. It felt a bit like deja vu, as she been in this position before.

"Now, Julia. Do you want to start by explaining to me why you broke into Larry's old office," Hewitt said.

She opened her mouth to speak but before anything came out, the door swung open and another police officer popped his head around the door.

"Yes! What is it?" Hewitt asked impatiently.

"There's a Clyde Chance here to see you. He has a lawyer with him. He was most insistent."

Julia's heart skipped a beat.

She was free! Clyde had managed it all, with the help of Kadi. She breathed in the fresh air as she walked arm in arm with her daughter, towards his car.

"I cannot believe you did it!" Kadi cried.

Clyde turned around and flashed them both a film star smile. "It was easy. I have the best lawyer in the business."

Julia rolled her eyes at him. "You're very modest too, Mr Chance."

"I am, aren't I. It's what I'm famed for."

"He really is a good lawyer. I was fascinated."

"Was he really, mum?" Kadi asked.

"Very," she replied, stroking her daughter's hair.

"I told you he would be with dating," she whispered.

"Let's not move too fast," she whispered back.

"Why don't I buy you both lunch? You must be hungry!" Clyde called over his shoulder.

"Yes, please. I'm starving," Julia said, rubbing her stomach.

"As long as it's somewhere better than Ivy Kinlaw's place," Kadi said.

"Did you not like it?" Julia asked.

"No, it's not a patch on your food. I don't think you have to worry about any competition from her."

"That's coming from someone who knows her food," Clyde said with a laugh.

They were half way through lunch when Julia suddenly remembered the blue carpet fibers she plucked from under Larry's desk. She reached into her pocket and held them up, much to Kadi's alarm, sitting next to her.

"I found these under Larry's desk," she said. "Could be a clue or then again, it might be something and nothing."

"What are they?" Clyde said from across the table, with a frown of concentration.

"They are carpet fibers, stained with some kind of blue substance."

"Doesn't prove very much," Kadi said gloomily. "It could be anything."

"You never know. It could just be the winning formula," Clyde said, winking at Julia.

"I'm going to take them to Tegan's lab to have them analysed. His death could have had something to do with his sudden turn for science."

"It seems like there must have been a quarrel in his office and whatever that is, was spilled on the carpet during it," Clyde said.

CHAPTER
SEVENTEEN

"Do you want us to wait for you, mum?" Kadi asked as they were all sitting in Clyde's car outside the lab.

"No, you two go on, I won't be long. I could do with a walk. I need to think about the case."

She stepped out of the car and blew a kiss to her daughter as Clyde drove away.

When she went inside the building the foyer was empty and there was nobody behind the reception desk this time. She could have heard a pin drop, it was so eerily quiet.

A sudden noise caught her ear coming from the lab room and she noticed the door was ajar. She slowly walked towards it and popped her head round to see inside. Tegan was there with her back to her and she was squeezing some liquid into a test tube, wearing the goggles she'd seen on her head the last time she was here.

"Hello, Tegan," Julia said softly, stepping further into the room.

Tegan spun around on the stool she was sitting on and the breath caught in Julia's throat as she saw the colour of the liquid she had been working with.

It was light blue! Just like on the carpet fibers.

Everything began to come clear to her. She tried to speak but she couldn't find her voice just then.

"What's wrong?" Tegan asked, sounding casual.

She couldn't reply.

"Don't worry, I'm not angry with you for sneaking in here, though I should be."

"Is that the secret formula you were working on when Larry took such an interest?" She asked at last, finding her voice.

"He wanted me to tell him all about my formulas but I turned him down. He was just after money."

"Oh, yes, that's right. You said he only cared about money."

"Yes, I did. What can I do for you?" She walked behind Julia and stood by the door.

Julia turned to face her with a look of determination upon her face. "You and Larry had a quarrel in his office the day before the fair, didn't you?"

Tegan's lips parted as if she was about to speak and there was a look of guilt on her face as she closed them again and shook her head.

"It's no use trying to deny it, Tegan. I know you did and what's more, I know what it was about. It was about that blue liquid over there." She pointed over her shoulder at the tubes of liquid sitting on the desk.

A look of anger came into Tegan's face for a moment and she slammed the door shut, locking it and placing the key in the pocket of her white coat. She then turned to Julia and folded her arms. "That blue liquid you speak so casually about, is a cure for a terrible disease. A disease my mother is at this moment rotting away in a nursing home with. Alzheimer's."

"It can cure patients with early onset of the disease and save others from the that terrible fate. My mother doesn't even know who I am anymore! That monster was going to take it all away from me!" Her voice was angry and full of tears.

"The lab or the formula?"

"He wanted everything. Tim and I were trying to keep it secret until I could get it out there. Larry Vallejo came and stole the formula and he was going to pass it off as his own creation. Imagine that!"

"You wanted the credit for yourself?"

"It wasn't about that. He only wanted it for

money. In the wrong hands it would have been corrupted. It would have gone to right places, but he didn't care about people. He cared about himself that was all and saving his lousy business."

"So you went to get the formula he'd stolen back and when he refused, you quarrelled? He spilled a little of the liquid and you didn't notice it had stained the carpet?" She held up the carpet fibers she had found.

"That's how it happened, yes."

"Then you confronted him again at the fair?"

"Yes, I needed to persuade him to give it back."

"But he refused and you decided to poison him. How did you do it?"

"I had already planned to kill him that day, if he didn't give it back." She walked around as she explained. "I put the Arsenic in a bottle of beer. I Knew he liked his beer and I enticed him with the bottle. He drank it all without question. No doubt he thought it was some kind of ploy to win him over."

"And everything tasted foul after that because he could still taste the Arsenic."

"I guess." She shrugged her shoulders.

"But why did you try to frame me, Tegan?" She asked, getting angry now.

Tegan frowned. "Oh, the pastry. That was just a last minute panic, I'm afraid. It was either you or

Ivy. I figured you being new here it would go down much better. Sorry." She sounded genuine enough, until she suddenly sprang to her desk and pulled out a syringe full of some nasty substance and waved it at her.

"I'm sorry about this too. It's the only way if I'm to make headway with my formula." She sprang towards her aiming the needle at her neck. To her relief, the door flew open and in walked DCI Hewitt, followed by P.C. Bird. They both tackled Tegan and knocked the syringe out of her hand. It was picked up by Sapphire, who made a sudden appearance in the room.

"Sapphy!" Julia cried. "What on earth are you doing here?"

"A sudden brain wave. Today, I remembered something Tegan had said to me once, about how she would do anything to save her lab and the formula she was working on. It kept going round and round my head until, at last, I had to check it out."

"I'm so glad you did," Julia replied, embracing her.

CHAPTER EIGHTEEN

K adi was standing outside the cottage, her bags on the floor at the ready. She had a glum look on her face as Julia locked up and walked to the car with her.

"Well, who'd have thought it? Kadi being sad to leave Devonshire."

"I thought it would be boring here," she said sadly.

"It was never that, was it?"

"Anything but. I found it all exciting, helping you solve a mystery."

"Hm. It isn't the word I would have chosen, but never mind. You can come back and visit when you've finished your studies."

"I can't wait. Will you see Clyde again?" She

looked up at her mother as she was about to climb into the car.

"I may do, though I think we'll take things steady for a while. I'm not sure I'm ready, yet."

Kadi got in the passenger seat and Julia closed the door behind her.

"Cooie!" Came a voice from next door.

Julia turned to see Ivy waving to her from over the hedge. "Cooie to you, too, Ivy."

"It wasn't either of us, then, as it turned out. We might have known the outcome, really. These scientists are all mad."

Julia shielded her face from the sun with her arm. "I suppose they are."

"I just wanted you to know there are no hard feelings, though it's business as usual where the food is concerned."

"Alright. Let the battle commence. May the best woman win and all that."

"Alright, dear." She waved again and disappeared back behind the hedge.

Julia shook her head. "Until next time....."

Manufactured by Amazon.ca
Bolton, ON